SEN SUPERPOWERS

The Classroom Mystery

a book about ADHD

Written by
Dr. Tracy Packiam Alloway

Illustrated by
Ana Sanfelippo

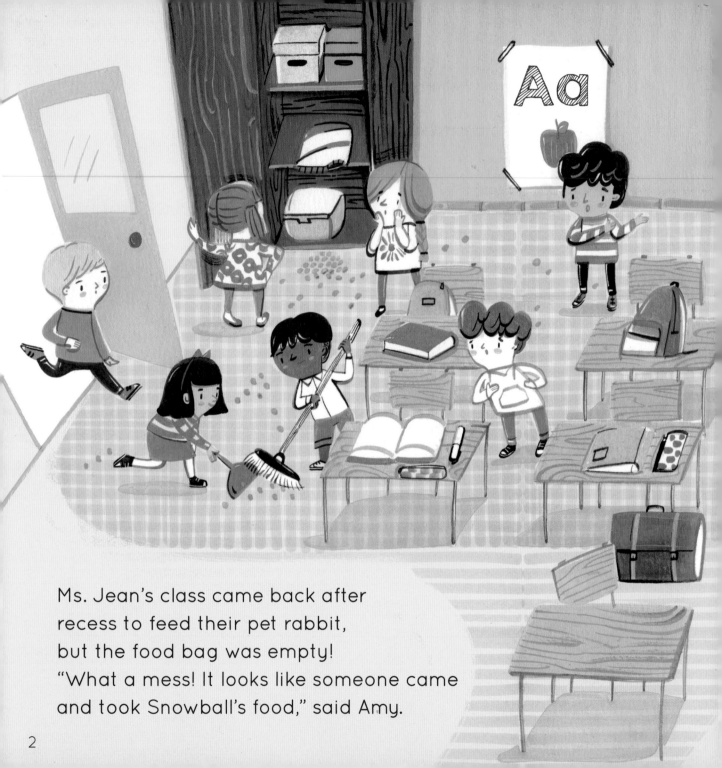

Ms. Jean's class came back after
recess to feed their pet rabbit,
but the food bag was empty!
"What a mess! It looks like someone came
and took Snowball's food," said Amy.

"Who would do something like that?" asked David.

Izzy thought about Snowball. "I want to help," she said loudly. "I'll be a detective and find out who took Snowball's food!"

3

But before Izzy could begin her detective work, the bell rang and Ms. Jean walked in. "Excuse me, Ms. Jean," said Izzy, raising her hand and tapping her foot loudly.

"Not now, Izzy. Let's get started and I'll answer questions at the end," said Ms. Jean.

4

Izzy tried to focus, but Ms. Jean sounded like a robot and the numbers on the board danced around and around.

$$3 + 2 =$$
$$5 \times 7 + 2 =$$
$$4 \times 4 =$$
$$1 + 6 =$$
$$2 + 10 =$$

All Izzy could think about was solving the rabbit food mystery.

Izzy wiggled in her seat.

She drummed her
fingers on her desk.

She chewed her pencil.

And she snapped her
hair clip on and off.

8

"I know I can solve this mystery," Izzy whispered.

"I think better when I'm high up." She climbed on top of her desk.

CRASH! Her books flew everywhere.

"Please try to settle down, Izzy," said Ms. Jean, gently.

Back in her chair, Izzy felt a breeze coming from the classroom window. "Ms. Jean said it was too hot earlier and opened the window... maybe the thief came in from outside?" she thought.

Izzy jumped up and rushed over to the window. The rest of the class followed, and they peered out onto the playground.

"What on earth is going on, class?
What are you looking at?" said Ms. Jean.
"We're looking for clues, Ms. Jean! Someone stole Snowball's food!" replied Izzy.

Izzy tried to think clearly. She closed her eyes and hummed loudly as she tried to put the pieces of the puzzle together.

"Izzy, what's wrong?" said Riley. "I remember hearing rustling in the bushes at recess," she said.

"Okay, class. Let's take
a break and investigate!"
said Ms. Jean.

Izzy led everyone across the playground toward the bushes. As they approached, Izzy noticed a trail of crumbs on the path.

"Look!" she cried. "Those crumbs look like Snowball's food—the thief must have been here!" said Izzy.

14

They peeked into the bushes and they searched high and low, but the thief was gone.

"It's no use, we'll never solve the mystery," moaned Riley.

But Izzy wasn't giving up yet.
She focused on the problem and
thought carefully about everything
she had heard that day.

Then she remembered something else...

On her way into school, she'd overheard
the janitor telling the principal that he'd
seen a squirrel in the shed yesterday.
Could it be another clue?

Izzy marched over to the shed. From the corner of her eye, she spotted a squirrel by the trunk of a big tree, nibbling on a pile of rabbit food.

"Look!" squealed Izzy. "That naughty squirrel is the food thief! He must have come in through the window, stolen Snowball's food from the cupboard, and taken it here to eat!"

Caught red-handed, the squirrel scampered
up the trunk to the top of the tree.

"Izzy, you did it!"
shouted Ben.
"How did you know where
to look?" Riley asked.

"I just thought really hard about
everything that happened today," said
Izzy, "and I pieced the clues together."

"Well done, Izzy! You solved the mystery!"
said Ms. Jean. "Now let's go back to the
classroom and give Snowball a snack."

NOTES FOR PARENTS AND TEACHERS

ADHD is a common learning difficulty that can cause problems with certain abilities, such as:

INHIBITION
Children with ADHD usually have poor inhibition and can struggle to control inappropriate behavior, thoughts, and speech. They can be impulsive and impatient, doing or thinking about the wrong things at the wrong time. For example, children may get up and walk around during a test, talk excessively, or interrupt others.

ATTENTION
Children with ADHD often have difficulties when they have to focus their attention on activities that they find long and boring. They may have trouble monitoring their actions and remembering instructions, losing sight of what they need to accomplish.

KEEPING STILL
ADHD is associated with fidgeting, hyperactivity, and restlessness. When children with ADHD get an urge to get up and walk around, or let their thoughts wander, they struggle to suppress the urge.

Try to consider the suitability of tasks that you give to a child with ADHD. They might have poor inhibition and struggle to keep still, but, just like Izzy, children with ADHD have strong verbal working memory. This skill means that they are great at remembering things that they hear. Some children with ADHD can also become hyperfocused, meaning that they are able to direct their attention to a single task that they find interesting, becoming so absorbed with it that they don't notice anything or anyone around them.

DISCUSSION POINTS ABOUT THE STORY

Explain to the children what ADHD is and how children with ADHD can find it hard to focus on their work and get along with others. Also talk about the many positive aspects of having ADHD, such as being energetic, spontaneous, and good at problem-solving. Below are some discussion points about the story that will help children with their comprehension skills as well as developing their awareness of ADHD:

(pp5-7) Izzy struggled to concentrate and sit still in class. Why do you think she found it hard? Have you ever struggled to focus during classes at school?

(p10) Izzy saw connections others missed and she was good at thinking outside the box. What were the clues? How did she use them to figure out who stole the food?

(pp8-9) Izzy climbed on top of her desk. Why do you think she acted this way? What do you think the rest of the class was thinking?

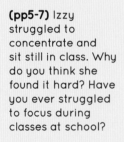

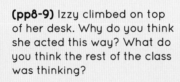

(pp20-21) How do you think Izzy felt at the end of the story after she solved the mystery? How do you think her friends felt? What about Ms. Jean?

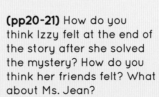

TIPS FOR BOOSTING MEMORY SKILLS

Here are some handy tips and ideas to help children be superheroes like Izzy!

TIME BURSTS

To boost concentration, short bursts of effort, such as 5 to 10 minutes, are better than a prolonged length of time.

CONNECT ACTIONS

Suggest that children try doing a physical action when learning to connect the action with the information. When they need to recall the information, they should perform the action and trigger their memory.

STUDY INTERMITTENTLY

If a child is reviewing for an exam, it can be effective to study intermittently, rather than at a set time each week.

WHERE WERE YOU?

When children are trying to remember information, encourage them to think of where they were when they learned it. What time of day was it? What were they wearing? These questions should help trigger their memory.

Quarto is the authority on a wide range of topics.

Quarto educates, entertains and enriches the lives of our readers—enthusiasts and lovers of hands-on living.

www.quartoknows.com

Author: Dr. Tracy Packiam Alloway
Illustrator: Ana Sanfelippo
Editors: Rachel Moss and Emily Pither
Designers: Clare Barber and Victoria Kimonidou
Consultant: Lorraine Petersen OBE

© 2019 Quarto Publishing plc

First published in 2019 by QEB Publishing,
an imprint of The Quarto Group.
6 Orchard Road, Suite 100
Lake Forest, CA 92630
T: +1 949 380 7510
F: +1 949 380 7575
www.QuartoKnows.com

A CIP record for this book is available from the Library of Congress.

ISBN 978-1-78603-580-6

Manufactured in Guangdong, China TT122019
9 8 7 6 5 4 3 2

FSC MIX
Paper from responsible sources
www.fsc.org FSC® C016973

To my eagle-eyed superhero Marcus, who loves to solve puzzles.